POPOKI
THE HAWAIIAN CAT
An Amazing Adventure
with the Whale

Written by
Diana C. Gleasner

Illustrated by
Andrea Evans Winton

Aloha Nui Loa
to
William Clark Gleasner

May all your dreams come true

Diana and Bill Gleasner
7994 Holly Court, Denver, NC 28037 U.S.A.
TEL: (704) 483-9301 FAX: (704) 483-6309
www.gleasner.com

Library of Congress Control Number: 2004100119
ISBN # 0-9651185-7-6

Marjorie Storch Graphic Design, Charlotte, NC

Printed in China by Everbest Printing Co, Ltd.

"Wake up, Leilani. Wake up, Mr. Cat."

Popoki did not want to wake up. He didn't like to be told what to do. He especially did not like Cousin Kai calling him Mr. Cat. Besides, it was still black outside.

Leilani jumped out of bed. She loved visiting her Aunty and cousin Kai on Maui. Having Popoki travel with her made this trip special. Aunty promised to drive them to the top of Mt. Haleakala so they could ride their bikes all the way down the great mountain.

At the top of the mountain, an icy wind blew. A few people huddled under blankets waiting for the sunrise. Popoki had never been so cold. He wished he were back home on Kauai where it was warm. When he shivered, Kai laughed.

"Welcome to Haleakala. In Hawaiian it means 'House of the Sun.' Look. Here comes the sun."

Fiery rays peeked over the edge of the huge crater.
Popoki wanted to watch the sun rise, but Kai was in a hurry.

Leilani wrapped Popoki in a small blanket and tucked him into her bike basket.

"All you have to do is steer and use your brakes," Kai said. "And keep your mouth closed, or you'll be eating pineapple bugs for breakfast."

Popoki kept his mouth shut, but his eyes were wide open. Sailing down the mountain made his fur tingle. They passed a blur of horses and cows. Popoki felt important flying by in his very own basket.

Halfway down the mountain, they stopped to eat sandwiches. "Now don't wander off," warned Kai. Popoki did not like being told what to do. While Kai and Leilani 'talked story,'* Popoki went exploring.

*"talk story" is island slang for "chatting"

At a protea farm, an old woman stopped gathering flowers to look him over. "Well, aren't you a fine popoki," she said. Finally, Popoki felt warm, inside and out.

He pounced on a gecko, but a big black cat appeared out of nowhere and went after the same gecko. The big black cat was mad. He jumped Popoki and scratched his nose.

Popoki howled. Leilani heard him and found him hiding
among the protea plants. "You've got to listen, Popoki, because,
if you don't, you're going to get into BIG trouble."

When they reached Aunty's house in Makawao, Kai said,
"Well, Mr. Cat, are you going to Hana with us tomorrow?"

Why didn't Kai call him by his real name?

"I know a rock pool near Hana where we can swim," Kai said.
"Mom is going to let me drive." He proudly showed Leilani his
new driver's license. Leilani was impressed. Popoki was not.

On the road to Hana they stopped to watch windsurfers dance on the waves like giant butterflies.

Kai said the road to Hana had 54 bridges and more than 600 curves. Yuk! The curves made Popoki feel sick. Kai drove too fast, and the road seemed to go on forever.

"Mr. Cat doesn't look so good," said Kai.

"Why don't you call him Popoki?" asked Leilani.

Kai laughed. "Popoki is Hawaiian for cat. So it's the same thing."

Popoki didn't think it was the same at all. Besides, Kai was the Hawaiian word for ocean, but no one called Kai anything but Kai.

When they spread out a picnic beside a splashy waterfall, Popoki didn't feel like eating so he tried catching fish. It was great fun until he fell into the water, and Kai had to pull him out.

"I told you not to go so close to the edge," said Leilani.

Popoki didn't like being wet, but he also didn't like being told what to do. What a long day! Popoki's head was spinning.

"Tomorrow, we will have our best adventure of all," promised Kai. "We're going to Lahaina to go whale watching."

Popoki had always had a lively interest in fish, but he soon learned whales were not fish. The captain of the boat said that whales were mammals. They were huge – bigger than a bus.

"These humpback whales spend their summers eating in Alaska," the captain explained, "and their winters having babies in Hawaii."

Enormous whales slapped their tails on the water. Some shot completely out of the ocean like rockets before crashing back into the water. Popoki could not believe his eyes.

"Look!" shouted the captain. "A mother whale is heading straight for us. And she has her young calf with her." Everyone rushed to see. The mother whale was almost as long as the boat.

The baby poked his head up and looked around. "We call that 'spyhopping'," said the captain. Then the mother came alongside the boat and floated on the water's surface.

The baby whale popped up beside its mother and stared straight at Popoki. Wow! Popoki would never forget the puzzled look in that baby whale's eye. He looked as if he had never seen a cat before.

"Stay back," warned Leilani. But Popoki wanted to get a better look. He leaned way over the side. The deck was slippery, and Popoki's paws were wet.

He fell out of the boat and landed – *plunk* – on the mother whale's back. "Cat overboard!" shouted Kai.

Someone threw a line. Popoki tried to hang onto it, but the line was moving and so was the mother whale. Popoki was scared.

The captain tried to reach him with a boat hook. Popoki
almost snared it, but it slipped out of his wet paws. He tried
again but missed.

"Hang onto my feet!" yelled Kai.

Leilani grabbed one leg. A man beside her grabbed the other. In one swift move, Kai swooped down, but Popoki was just out of reach. Slowly the mother whale began to sink.

Popoki's paws were covered with water.

"Jump, Popoki, jump!" called Leilani. Popoki jumped as high as he could. Kai grabbed him by one paw and hauled him into the boat.

Back home in Aunty's kitchen, Kai and Leilani told the story over and over. Aunty had many questions. She called Leilani's mother on Kauai so Leilani could tell her about the whale.

Aunty gave Popoki a bowl of fresh mahimahi. The fish tasted better than ever before.

"I had to rescue Popoki," Kai said with a grin. "After all, he's my cousin." Popoki liked being called by his real name. "When Leilani said 'jump', oh boy, did you ever jump. For once you listened, and it saved your life."

Popoki began to wonder. What would have happened if Kai had not been so quick? But thinking made him tired.

What he needed right now was a nap.

Glossary

gecko - *gek-oh* - small lizard found in the Hawaiian Islands

Hana - *HAH-nah* - community on the island of Maui

Hawaii - *hah-WAI-ee* - islands in the Pacific Ocean - 50th state of U.S.A.

humpback whale - a species of whale found in the Hawaiian Islands
   and elsewhere

Kai - *kye* - boy's name, Hawaiian word for sea or ocean

Kauai - *Kau-(W)AH-ee* - one of the Hawaiian Islands

Lahaina - *Lah-HAI-na* - the old whaling port on the island of Maui

Leilani - *lay-LON-ee* - girl's name

Makawao - *MA-ka-WOW* - a cowboy town on island of Maui

mammal - animal that feeds its young milk

mahimahi - *ma-hee-ma-hee* - Hawaiian fish

Maui - *MOW-ee* - one of the Hawaiian Islands

Mt. Haleakala - *Mount HAH-lai-AH-ka-LAH* - dormant volcano on island
   of Maui; in Hawaiian 'Haleakala' means 'House of the Sun'

Popoki - *Po-po-kee* - Hawaiian word for cat

protea - *pro-TEE-a* - exotic tropical flower

spyhopping - head up, looking around

talk story - island slang for chatting

Author - Diana C. Gleasner

Diana had a longtime dream of one day living in Hawaii. She, her husband Bill, and their two children, Suzanne and Stephen, moved from Buffalo, New York, to the Hawaiian island of Kauai.

While the family was camping on Kauai's Na Pali coast, 12-year-old Suzanne Gleasner adopted a starving kitten. She named it Popoki. The kitten survived many adventures and became a much loved member of the family.

A writer for more than thirty years, Diana Gleasner has written thirty books as well as countless magazine and news-paper articles. She received a B.A. from Ohio Wesleyan University and M.A. from the State University of New York at Buffalo. The Gleasners now live in North Carolina.

Illustrator - Andrea Evans Winton

Andrea has been a freelance graphic artist, illustrator, and muralist for more than 25 years working in a variety of art related fields from gallery coordinator to custom framer. Her fine arts work has won numerous awards and is displayed in collections throughout the United States and United Kingdom.

Illustrating children's books is Andrea's lifelong dream. Her formal education was at Brooks Institute of Fine Arts in Santa Barbara, California, and through various workshops with world famous artists.

The Wintons currently reside in Mariposa, California - a quaint 49'er gold-mining town in the Sierra Foothills near Yosemite. However, the only real "gold" in her life comes in the form of painting a little yellow cat named Popoki. Andrea's true treasures are her Scottish-born husband, three children, four stepchildren, and ten grandchildren ... and to be able to share her art with all of them and others.

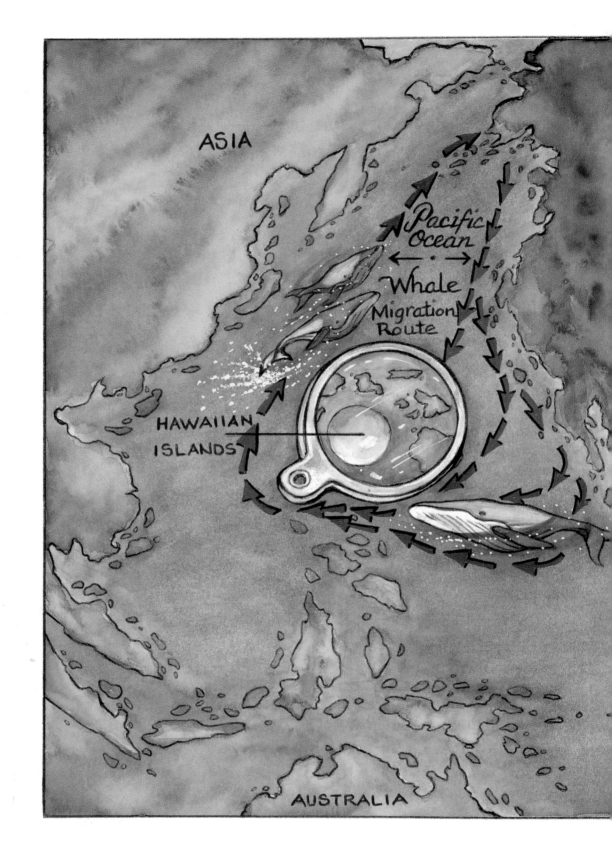